First Preschool Book

BASIC CONCEPTS

Contents

- Alphabets
- Numbers
- Shapes
- Colours
- Opposites
- Nursery Rhymes

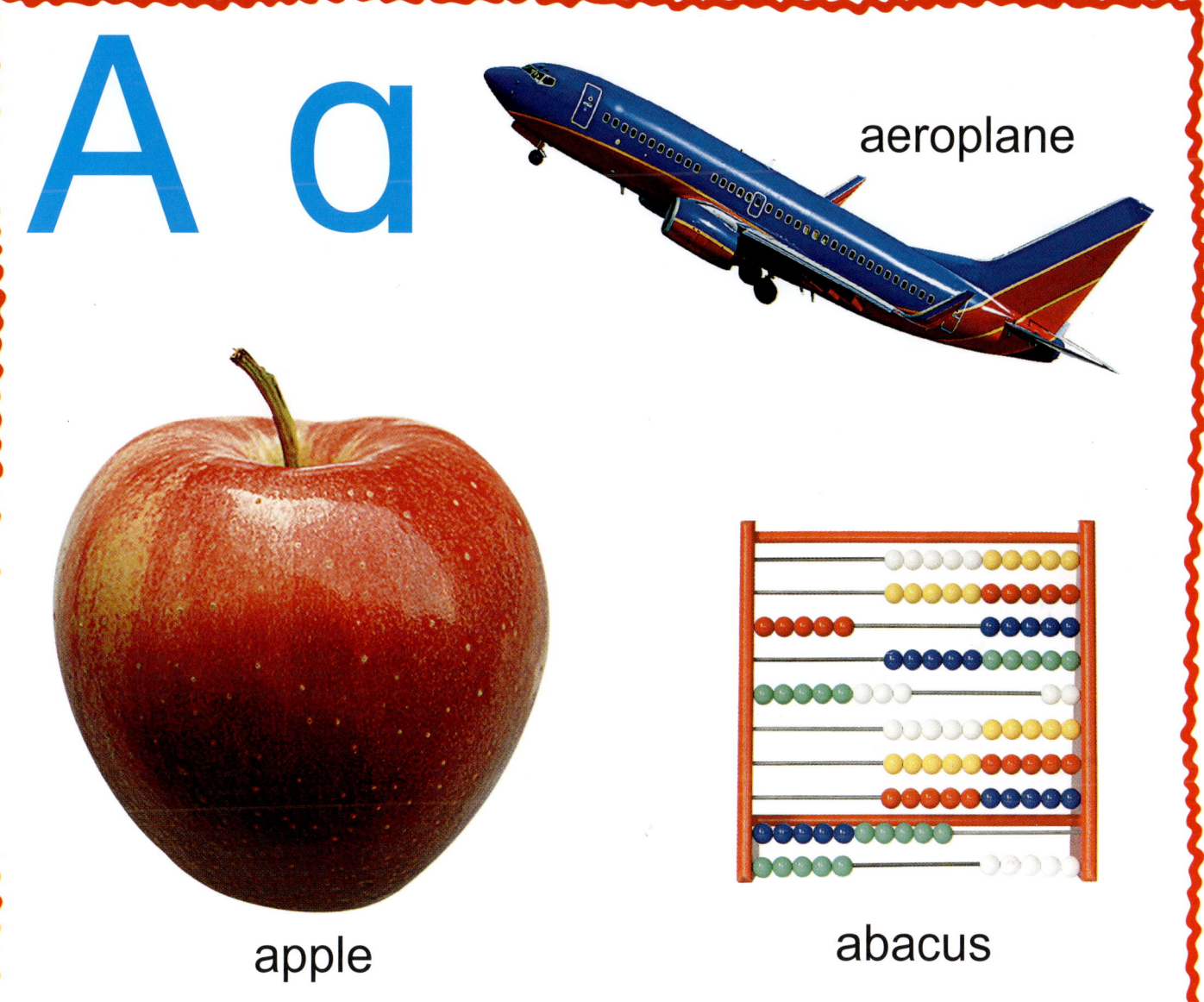

B b

ball

butterfly

bucket

C c

cat

cake

camera

D d

doll

door

dinosaur

E e

egg

eagle

eraser

F f

frock

fan

fruits

G g

globe

guitar

H h

hat

handbag

M m

mug

mask

N n

nest

necklace

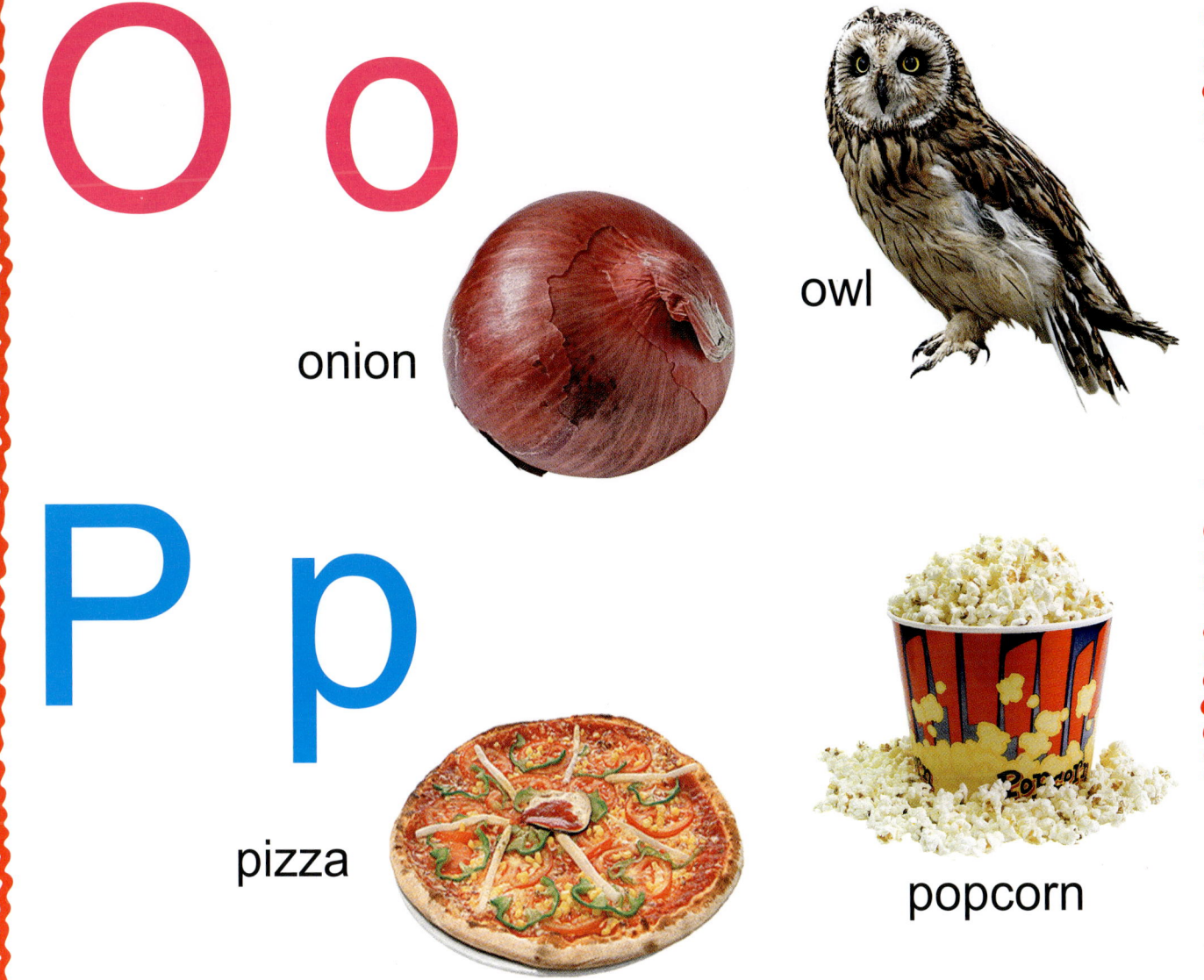

S s

swan

shoes

T t

trumpet

telephone

U u

umbrella

unicorn

V v

vest

van

W w

watch

watermelon

X x

xylophone

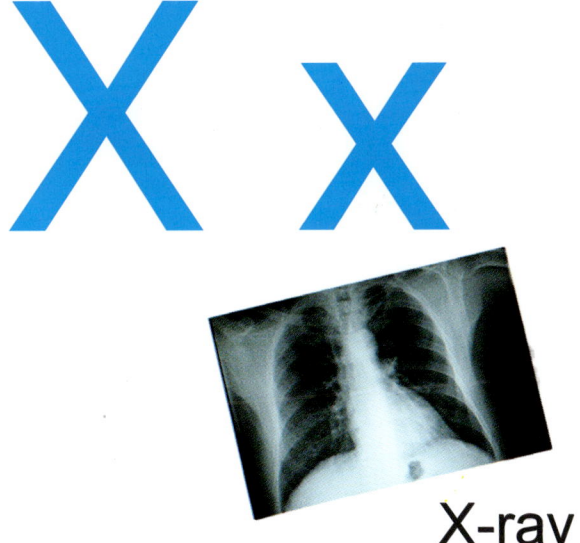

X-ray

Numbers

1 one

2 two

3 three

6
six

7
seven

8
eight

9
nine

10
ten

11
eleven

12
twelve

14
fourteen

15
fifteen

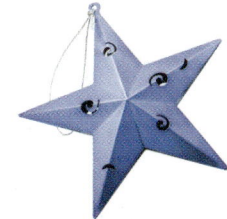

16
sixteen

17
seventeen

18
eighteen

19
nineteen

20
twenty

Shapes

Everything around us has a shape.

Here are some shapes.

circle

clock

pizza

tyre

triangle

signboard

watermelon

cheese

party hat

ring

bangles

ring

wreath

lifebuoy

painting

cushion

carrom board

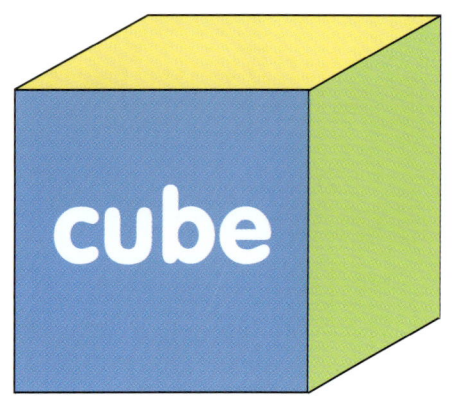

dice

Rubik's cube

sugar cube

ice cube

rectangle

door

map

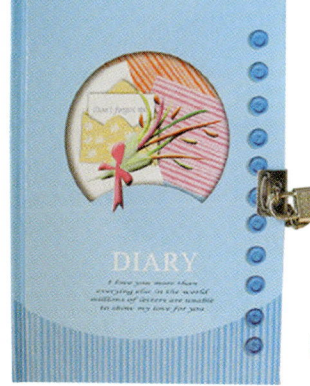
diary

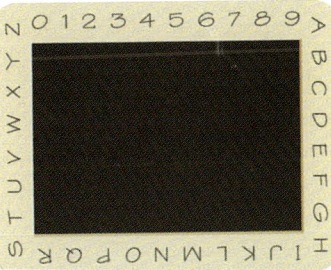
slate

sphere

cylinder

rolling pin

battery

soup can

fire extinguisher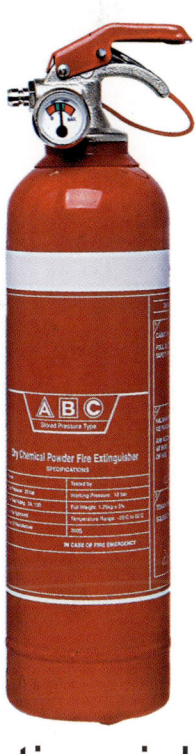

postbox

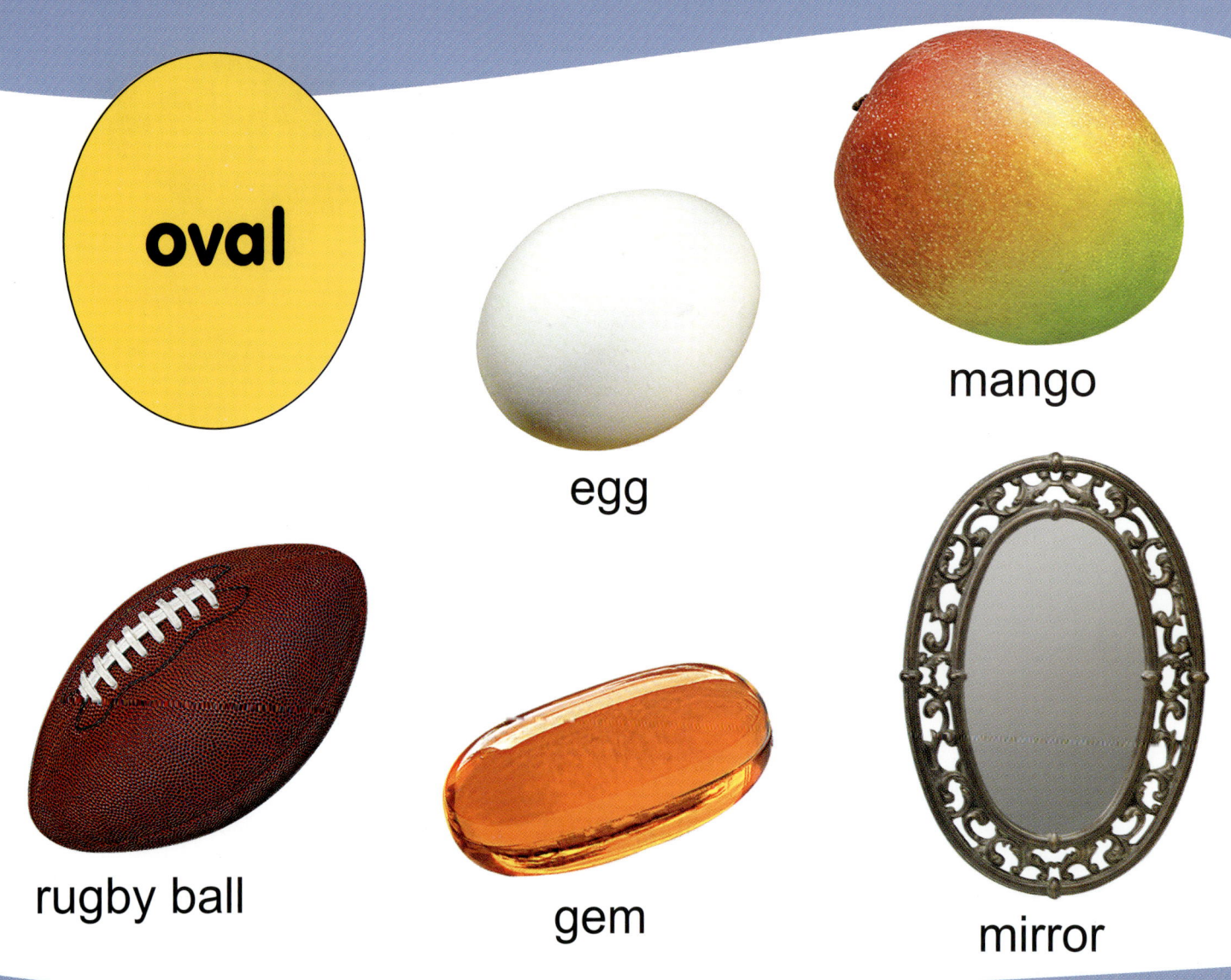

Match the shape

Name the shapes

Colours

blue

inkpot

bluebell

gumboots

duck

lemons

canary

taxi

pink

booties

hat

purple

towels

eggplant

orange

carrots

orange

white

milk

polar bear

Name all the colours you see on this page.

Opposites

big

small

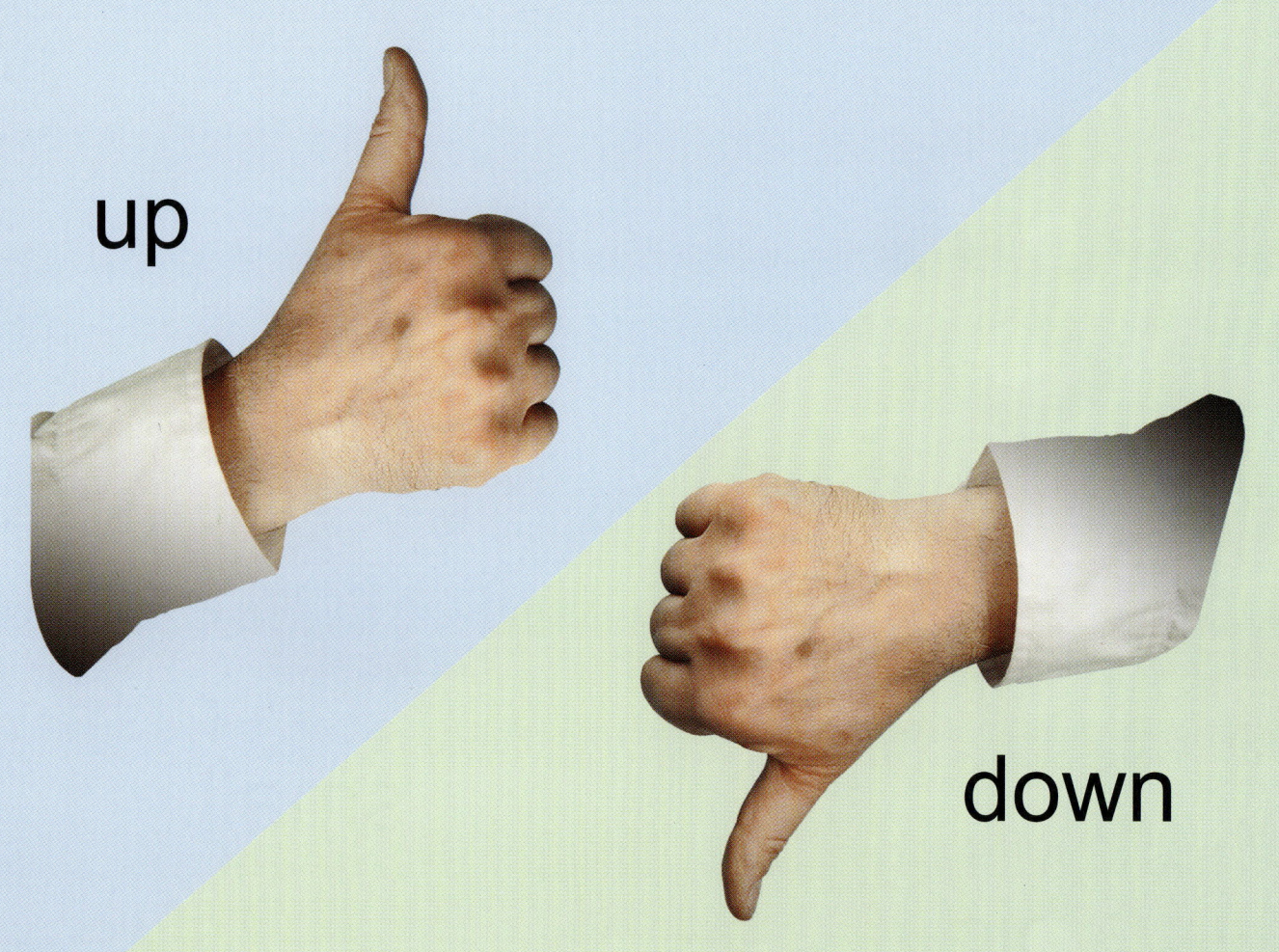

full

half

cold

hot

empty  full

happy

sad

one

many

sour

sweet

push

pull

short

tall

rough

smooth

dirty

clean

black

white

closed

open

in

out

fresh

stale

hard

soft

HICKETY, PICKETY

Hickety, pickety, my fine hen,
She lays eggs for gentlemen.
Gentlemen come every day
To see what my fine hen doth lay.
Sometimes nine and sometimes ten,
Hickety, pickety, my fine hen.

HICKORY, DICKORY, DOCK

Hickory, dickory, dock,
The mouse ran up the clock.
The clock struck one,
The mouse ran down,
Hickory, dickory, dock.

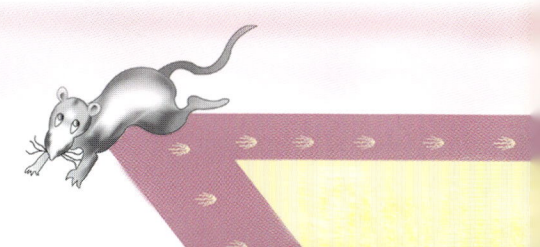

JACK AND JILL

Jack and Jill went up the hill,
To fetch a pail of water.
Jack fell down,
And broke his crown,
And Jill came tumbling after.

MARY HAD A LITTLE LAMB

Mary had a little lamb,
Its fleece was white as snow.
And everywhere that Mary went,
The lamb was sure to go.

PUSSYCAT, PUSSYCAT

Pussycat, pussycat,
Where have you been?
I've been to London
To look at the Queen.
Pussycat, pussycat,
What did you there?
I frightened a little mouse
Under her chair.

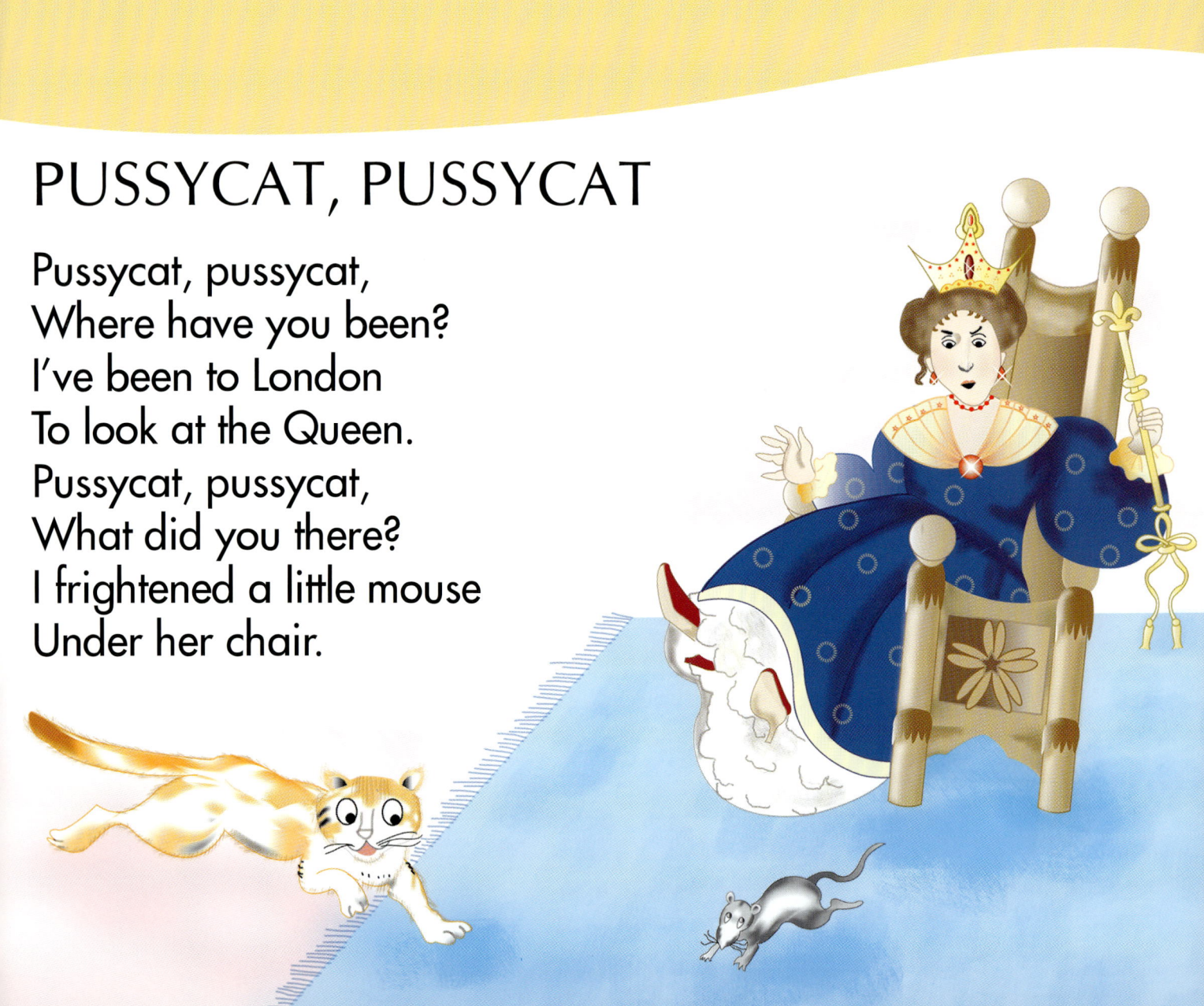

LITTLE JACK HORNER

Little Jack Horner
Sat in a corner,
Eating his Christmas pie.
He put in his thumb
And pulled out a plum,
And said, "What a
Good boy am I!"

THE FARMER IN THE DELL

The farmer in the dell,
The farmer in the dell,
Heigh ho! The derry-o!
The farmer in the dell.

The farmer takes a wife,
The farmer takes a wife,
Heigh ho! The derry-o!
The farmer takes a wife.
The wife takes a child, …
The child takes a dog, …
The dog takes a cat, …
The cat takes a mouse …

THREE LITTLE KITTENS

Three little kittens,
They lost their mittens,
And they began to cry,
"Oh Mother dear,
We sadly fear
Our mittens we have lost!"
"What! Lost your mittens,
You naughty kittens?
Then you shall have no pie!"

TWINKLE, TWINKLE

Twinkle, twinkle, little star,
How I wonder what you are!
Up above the world so high,
Like a diamond in the sky.

LITTLE MISS MUFFET

Little Miss Muffet
Sat on a tuffet,
Eating her curds and whey.
There came a big spider,
That sat down beside her,
And frightened
Miss Muffet away!

HEY, DIDDLE, DIDDLE!

Hey, diddle, diddle!
The cat and the fiddle,
The cow jumped over the moon.
The little dog laughed
To see such sport,
And the dish ran away
With the spoon.

PETER, PETER, PUMPKIN EATER

Peter, Peter, pumpkin eater,
Had a wife and couldn't keep her;
He put her in a pumpkin shell,
And there he kept her very well.

ONE, TWO

One, two,
Buckle my shoe.

Three, four,
Knock at the door.

Five, six,
Pick up sticks.

Seven, eight,
Lay them straight.

Nine, ten,
A big fat hen.

THERE WAS AN OLD WOMAN

There was an old woman
Who lived in a shoe.
She had so many children,
She didn't know what to do.

She gave them some broth,
Without any bread;
And whipped them all soundly
And put them to bed.

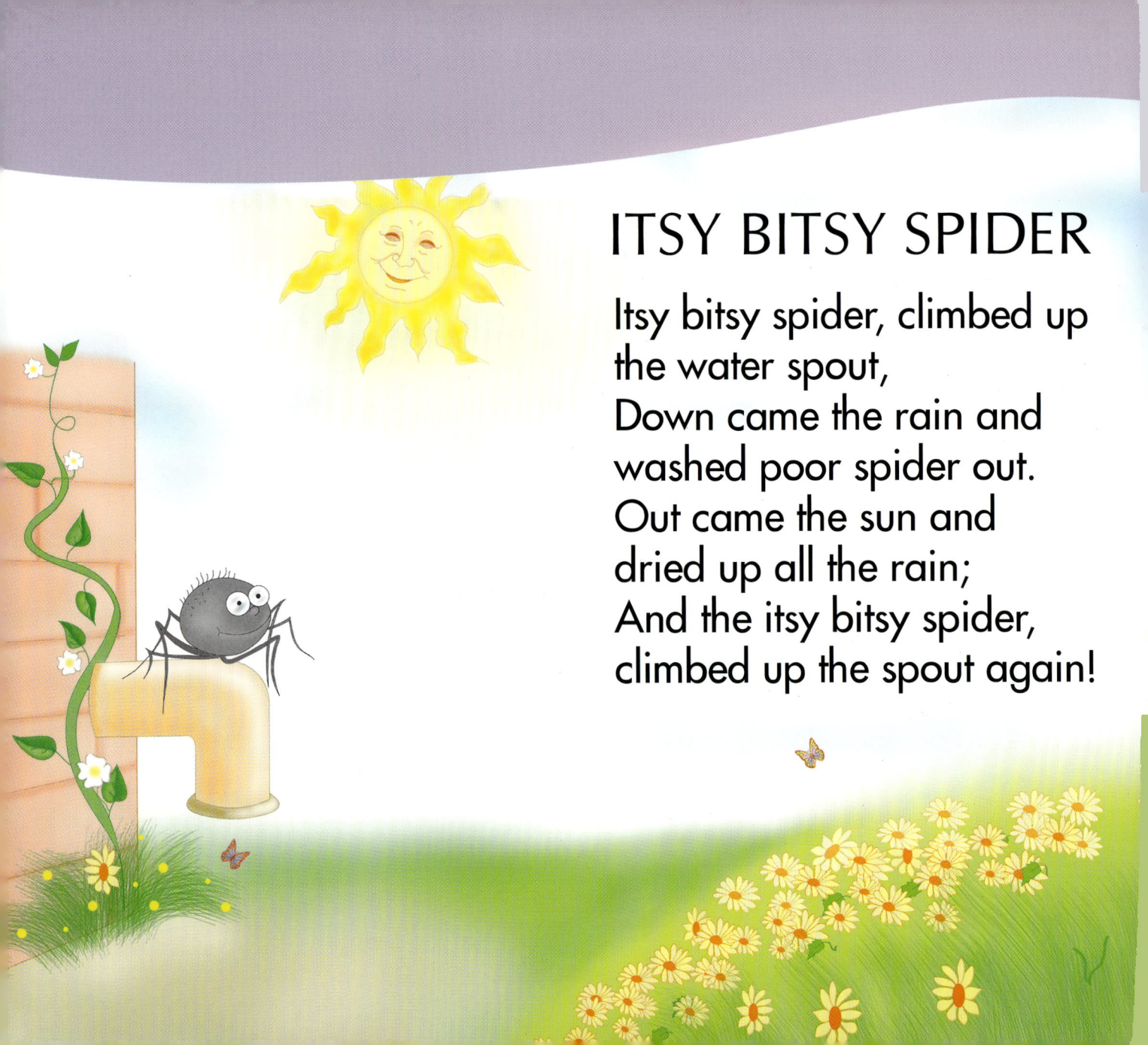

ITSY BITSY SPIDER

Itsy bitsy spider, climbed up the water spout,
Down came the rain and washed poor spider out.
Out came the sun and dried up all the rain;
And the itsy bitsy spider, climbed up the spout again!